The Twilight Princess

Written by Joe Duncombe

Illustrated by Cong Nguyen

When I was younger,
and after I had gone to bed,
I would wake up
from my dreams
at
the sound
of a giggling girl,
outside my window

I would get up
and look through the glass
to see her wearing
a white dress.

I would watch
her skip between trees
and dance
all around the park

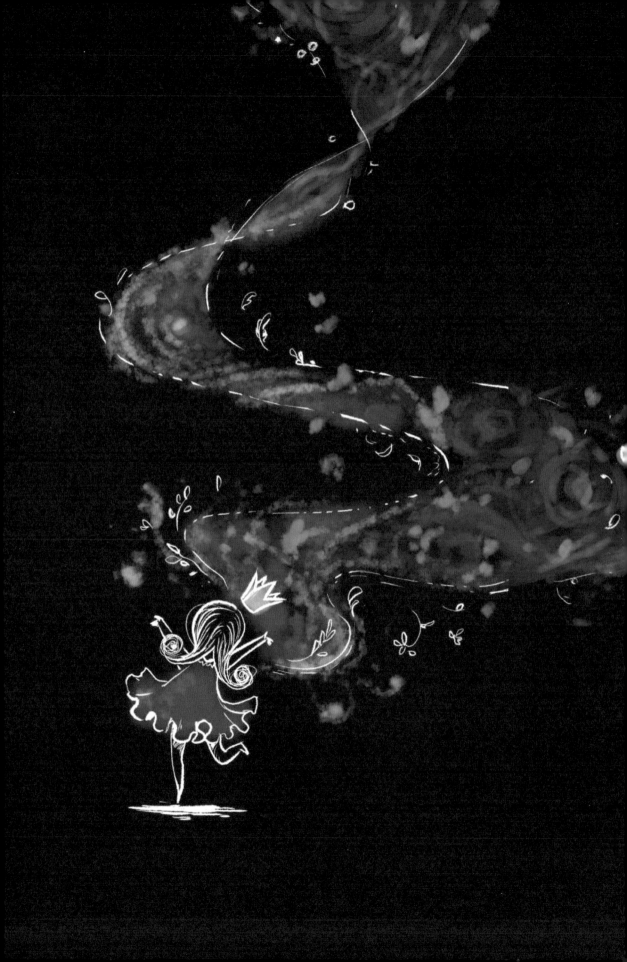

The girl would
swing on swings
and spin on
the merry-go-round
laughing
and smiling
all through the night.

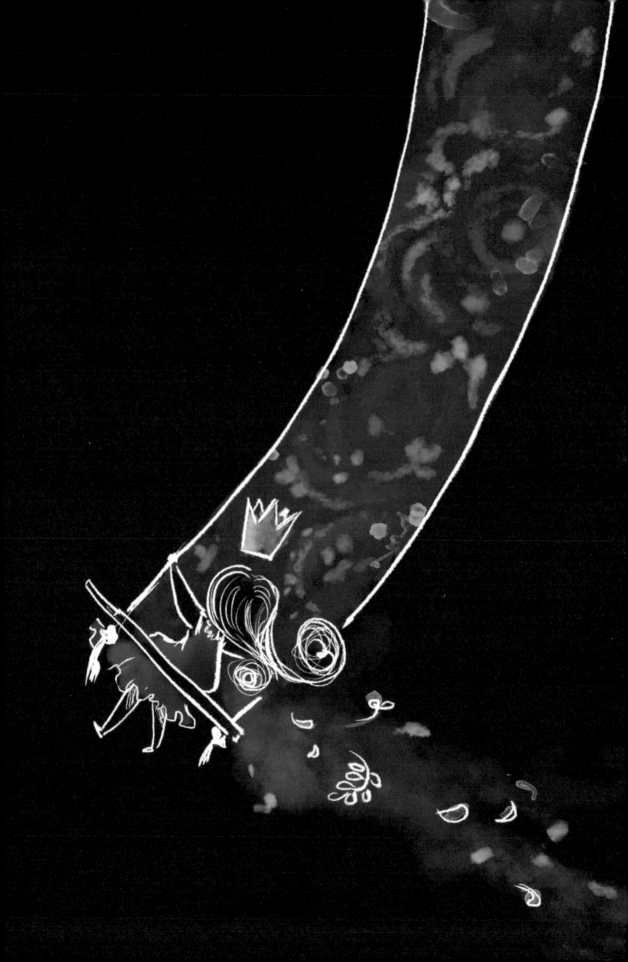

But every night,
when the girl would stand
in front of
the flowerbed,
she would stop
and look
all alone
and sad.

It was
the only time
she would not
smile.

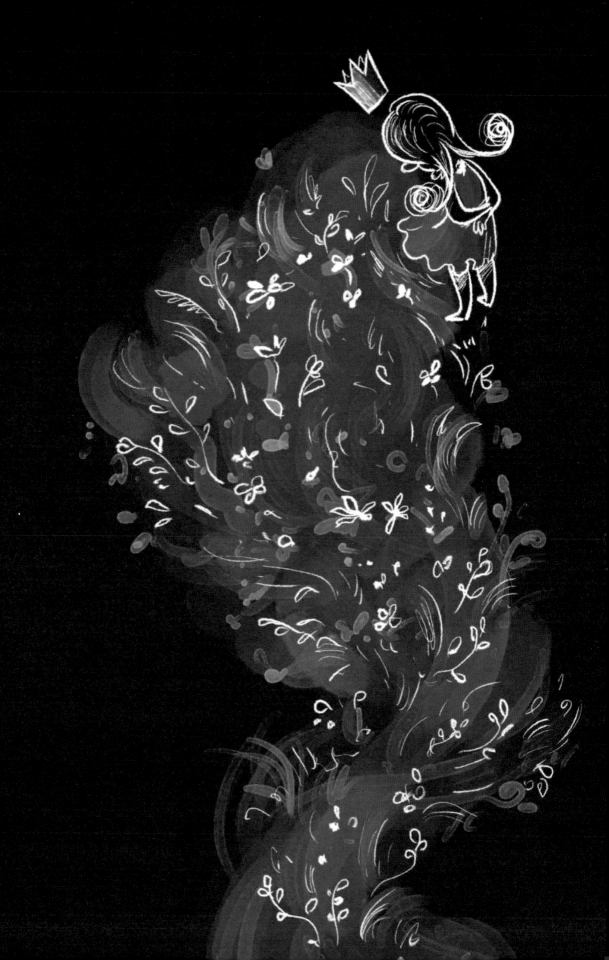

Under
the moon,
she
would look
at the flowers
and
cry.

It was on
one of those nights,
after I heard
her giggle.

I went
down to the park
and said
'Hello.'

We skipped
through the trees
and
laughed
as
we touched
the sky
on the swings

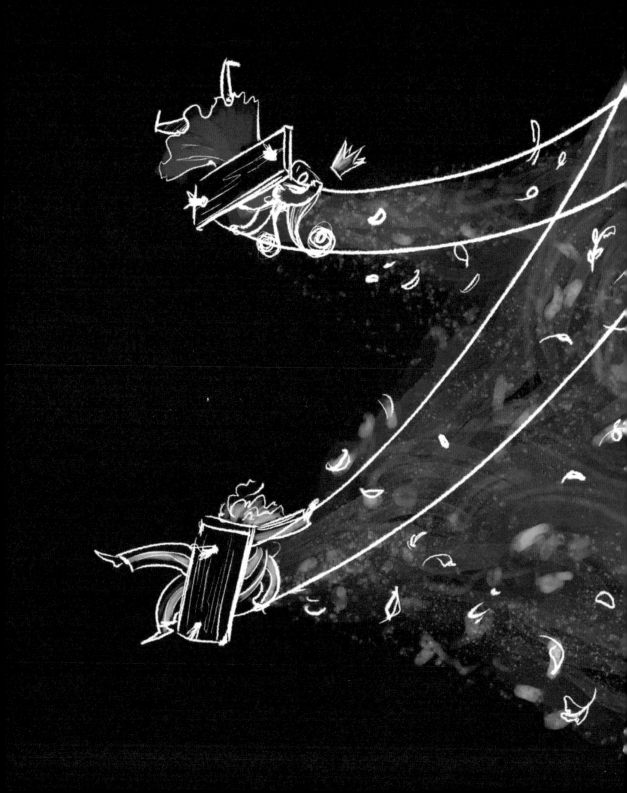

But
when we got
to the flowers,
again
she stopped.

When she
started to cry
I had to ask her,
"Why do they
make you
so sad?"

And then
she told me that
she was
a princess,
cursed
to never walk
in the sun..

She said
that she loved
looking at flowers,
but not once
had she seen
their
colours

The very next night,
when her laughter
filled the park,
I gave her
a gift
of
a large,
white
parasol.

She asked me
what it was
and
I told her,
"It's an umbrella
for the sun"
and that
tomorrow,
she could come out
and see
all of
the colours.

The next morning
I woke to
hear a girl
laughing
outside my window.
I watched
the girl in a
white dress
dance
through the park,
under a
large white
parasol

I left my room
and joined her
on the
merry-go-round,
spinning
and laughing
together.
But when we
got to
the flowerbed,
once again
she started to
cry.

The princess
told me
that she was
happy
and that these
were tears
of joy.
The colours
of all the flowers,
were the most
magical
thing she had
ever seen.

And then
she leant down
to get
a closer look
and
she reached out
to
touch
a petal

"Princess!
The sun shines
on your hand."

The girl looked
at her hand,
gently
holding a flower,
bathed in
golden
sun.

And she
kept her hand
there,
and she smiled
as the sun
didn't burn.

Just like that
the curse
was
no
more.

When I was
younger
and
the sun was
in the sky.

I would see
the twilight princess
looking at
the flowers
and
she was never
sad again

We hope you enjoyed the story

If you did please leave a review

And why not check out our other adventures

Thank you

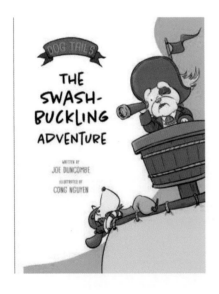

Dog Tails - The Swashbuckling Adventure

Available on Amazon

Flatbassetpublishing.com

Printed in Great Britain
by Amazon